This book belongs to:

_____

GOLDILOCKS
&
THE THREE BEARS

COLORED ILLUSTRATIONS

Allen D. Bragdon Publishers, Inc.
South Yarmouth, Massachusetts

Published by Allen D. Bragdon Publishers, Inc.
Tupelo Road, South Yarmouth, MA 02664

Originally published by M. A. Donahue & Company

Distributed to the book trade in the U.S. and Canada
by The Talman Company, New York

Manufactured in Hong Kong 1 2 3 4 5 6 7 8 9 10

Library of Congress-in-Publication Data
Goldilocks & the three bears.
    p.   cm.--(Bedtime classics library; 4)
    Summary: Lost in thewoods, a tired and hungry little girl finds the
house of the three bears where she helps herself to food and goes to sleep.
    ISBN 0-916410-55-2
    [1. Folklore.   2. Bears--Folklore.]   I. Goldilocks and the three
bears.   English.   II. Title: Goldilocks and the three bears   III. Seriers.
PZ8.1.G62   1991   398.21--dc20   [E]   90-46136

Goldilocks & The Three Bears

LITTLE Goldilocks was a pretty girl, who lived once upon a time in a far-off country.

One day she was sitting on the hearthrug playing with her two kittens, and you would have thought she was as happy as a queen, and quite contented to stay where she was, instead of wanting to run about the world meddling with other people's property.

But it happened that she was rather mischievous, and teased her pets, so one of them scratched her and then she would play with them no longer.

GOLDILOCKS & THE THREE BEARS

She got up and trotted away into the woods behind her mother's house, and it was such a warm, pleasant day that she wandered on and on until she came to a part of the woods where she had never been before.

GOLDILOCKS & THE THREE BEARS

Goldilocks stopped when she came to the Bears' house, and began to wonder who lived there.

"I'll just look in and see," she said, and so she did.

GOLDILOCKS & THE THREE BEARS

Now in this wood there lived a family of Three Bears. The first was a GREAT BIG BEAR, the second was a MIDDLE SIZED BEAR and the third was a *Little Teeny Tiny Bear,* and they all lived together in a funny little house, and very happy they were.

GOLDILOCKS & THE THREE BEARS

But there was no one there, for the Bears had all gone out for a morning walk, whilst the soup they were going to have for dinner cooled upon the table.

GOLDILOCKS & THE THREE BEARS

Goldilocks was rather hungry after her walk, and the soup smelt so good, that she began to wish the people of the house would come and invite her to have some.

But although she looked everywhere under the table and the cupboards, she could find no one.

At last she could resist no longer, but made up her mind to take just a little sip to see how the soup tasted.

The soup had been put into three bowls—a Great Big Bowl for the Great Big Bear, a Middling-Sized Bowl for the Middling-Sized Bear, and a Teeny Tiny Bowl for the Teeny Tiny Bear; beside each bowl lay a spoon.

GOLDILOCKS & THE THREE BEARS

Goldilocks took one and helped herself to a spoonful of soup from the Great Big Bowl.

Ugh! how it burnt her mouth; it was so hot with pepper that she did not like it at all; still, she was very hungry, so she thought she would try again.

This time she took a sip of the Middling-Sized Bear's soup, but she liked that no better for it was too salty. But when she tasted the Teeny Tiny Bear's soup it was just as she liked it; so she ate it all up.

GOLDILOCKS & THE THREE BEARS

When she had finished her dinner she noticed three chairs standing by the wall.

One was a Great Big Chair, and she climbed upon that and sat down. Oh, dear! how hard it was! She was sure she could not sit there long.

GOLDILOCKS & THE THREE BEARS

Then she climbed up on the next, which was only a Middling-Sized Chair, but that was too soft; so she went on to the last which was a Teeny Tiny Chair, and suited her exactly.

It was so comfortable that she sat on and on until if you'll believe it, she actually sat the bottom out. Then of course, she was comfortable no longer, so she got up and began to wonder what she would do next.

GOLDILOCKS & THE THREE BEARS

There was a staircase in the bears' house, and Goldilocks thought she would go up it and see where it led to.

So up she went, and when she reached the top she laughed outright, for the bears' bedroom was the funniest she had ever seen.

In the middle of the room stood a Great Big Bed, on one side of it there was a Middling-Sized Bed, and on the other was a Teeny Tiny Bed.

GOLDILOCKS & THE THREE BEARS

Goldilocks was sleepy, so she thought she would lie down and have a little nap. First she got upon the Great Big Bed, but it was just as hard as the Great Big Chair had been; so she jumped off and tried the Middling-Sized Bed, but it was so soft that she sank right down into the feather cushions and was nearly smothered.

GOLDILOCKS & THE THREE BEARS

"I will try the Teeny Tiny Bed," she said, and so she did, and it was so comfortable that she soon fell fast asleep.

Whilst she lay there, dreaming of all sorts of pleasant things, the three bears came home from their walk very hungry and quite ready for their dinners.

But, Oh! dear me! how cross the Great Big Bear looked when he saw his spoon had been used and thrown under the table.

"WHO HAS BEEN TASTING MY SOUP?" he cried, in a Great Big Voice. "AND WHO HAS BEEN TASTING MINE?" cried the Middling-Sized Bear, in a Middling-Sized Voice.

"But who has been tasting mine and ate it all up?" cried the poor little Teeny Tiny Bear, in a Teeny Tiny Voice, with the tears running down his Teeny Tiny Face.

When the Great Big Bear went to sit down in his Great Big Chair, he cried out in his Great Big Voice: "WHO HAS BEEN SITTING ON MY CHAIR?"

GOLDILOCKS & THE THREE BEARS

And the Middling-Sized Bear cried in a Middling-Sized Voice: "WHO HAS BEEN SITTING ON MY CHAIR?" But the Teeny Tiny Bear cried out in a Teeny Tiny Voice of anger: *"Who has been sitting on my chair and sat the bottom out?"*

By this time the Bears were sure that someone had been in their house quite lately; so
they looked about to see if someone were not
there yet.

There was certainly no one downstairs, so
they went up the staircase to their bedroom.

As soon as the Great Big Bear looked at his bed, he cried out in his Great Big Voice: **"WHO HAS BEEN LYING ON MY BED?"**

GOLDILOCKS & THE THREE BEARS

And the Middling-Sized Bear, seeing that the coverlet was all rumpled, cried out in a Middling-Sized Voice: "WHO HAS BEEN LYING ON MY BED?"

GOLDILOCKS & THE THREE BEARS

But the Teeny Tiny Bear cried out, in a Teeny Tiny Voice of astonishment: *"Who has been lying on my bed and lies there yet?"*

Now, when the Great Big Bear began to speak, Goldilocks dreamt that there was a bee buzzing in the room, and when the Middling-Sized Bear began to speak, she dreamt that it was flying out of the window.

But when the Teeny Tiny Bear began to speak, she dreamt that the bee had come back and stung her on the ear, and up she jumped. Oh! how frightened she was when she saw the three bears standing beside her.

GOLDILOCKS & THE THREE BEARS

She hopped out of bed and in a second was out through the open window, never stopping to wonder if the fall had hurt her.

She got up and ran and ran and ran, until she could go no farther, always thinking that the bears were close behind her. And then she found that in her fright, she had run straight home without knowing it.

GOLDILOCKS & THE THREE BEARS

And the three bears, although they often looked for her, never saw little Goldilocks again.

GOLDILOCKS & THE THREE BEARS

If you can find that same wood where the three bears lived, perhaps you can find their dear little house with the green door and *perhaps* you can find Goldilocks.

BEDTIME CLASSICS LIBRARY
Museum-quality reproductions of classic old editions in full color

Each of these volumes is at once a precious object of folk art, a classic storybook for a child to read or be read from, and a perfect gift for a child who will remember it always and pass it on as a family heirloom.

This is a genuine piece of Americana that must be enjoyed by a new generation of children. The Bedtime Classics Library is to be commended for its efforts in presenting treasured classics from the past to children of today.
—C. Clodfelter, Ph.D., Chairman, Department of Education, The University of Dallas

Little Red Riding Hood

The text is a retold version of the French *Le Petit Chaperon Rouge* collected by Charles Perrault in 1696 and originally published in his work entitled *The Tales of Mother Goose*. This retelling eliminates the violent details in the original French tale, so it is suitable for young children.

This heirloom facsimile is cloth-bound, sewn with sturdy thread, and has those lovely, old-fashioned drawings at every turn. The colors upon yellowed pages give this the warmth of an actual antique.
—Kristiana Gregory, *Los Angeles Times*
ISBN 0-916410-35-8

Peter Rabbit

On September 2, 1893, a British lady named Beatrix Potter wrote this story about a disobedient rabbit named Peter. When she mailed it to her young friend Noel Moore, she included some of her own drawings. Later she asked Noel's mother if she could have it back so she could revise it a little, add some more illustrations, and try to have it published. No one wanted it, so in December of 1901 she had 250 copies printed with the title *The Tale of Peter Rabbit*. This facsimile reproduces that story and the illustrations from an early edition.

ISBN 0916410-24-2

Three Little Pigs

An ideal edition to read aloud at bedtime. The text is short and a full-color, full-page picture faces each page of text. This holds the child's attention as each new page is turned and the story is soon finished.

The illustrations are indeed old-fashioned and charming, with muted colors and a style reminiscent of Caldecott, and the retelling is faithful to the oral tradition—School Library Journal

ISBN 0-916410-38-2

Distributed to the book trade by The Talman Company, New York

Allen D. Bragdon Publishers, Inc. Tupelo Road, South Yarmouth, MA 02664